The Magic of Christmas
Claire Freedman
Illustrated by
Gail Yerrill

The mice are out gathering holly,
As soft snowflakes swirl everywhere.
There are hushed little whispers
of Christmas,
And a magical feel in the air.

Little Mouse shares the excitement,
As he scampers about in the snow.
But what is the magic of Christmas?
That's what he's longing to know!

"It's sitting indoors," says Grandpa,
"And letting the fire thaw your toes.
It's the warm smell of baking and spices,
Deliciously tickling your nose."

His brother squeaks, "Building a snowman,
And patting the snow into place.
Then dressing him up in a hat and a scarf,
With raisins and nuts for his face."

"It's going outdoors
to make snowballs,
And throwing them all, one by one.
It's running away to hide by a tree—
The best part of
Christmas is fun!"

"It's sledding downhill," laugh his cousins,
"To land in the soft, sparkling snow.
It's skating and sliding out on the ice.
The magic is how fast we go!"

His sister says, "Christmas means presents,
And bringing them home, secretly,
To wrap up in bright, shiny paper,
With big love and kisses from me."

"It's soft voices singing,"
says Grandma,
"Sweet carols—
all through the night.
With little ones
huddled together,
Warmed by our
lantern's bright light."

with love
x x x
to
dad
to dear
mommy

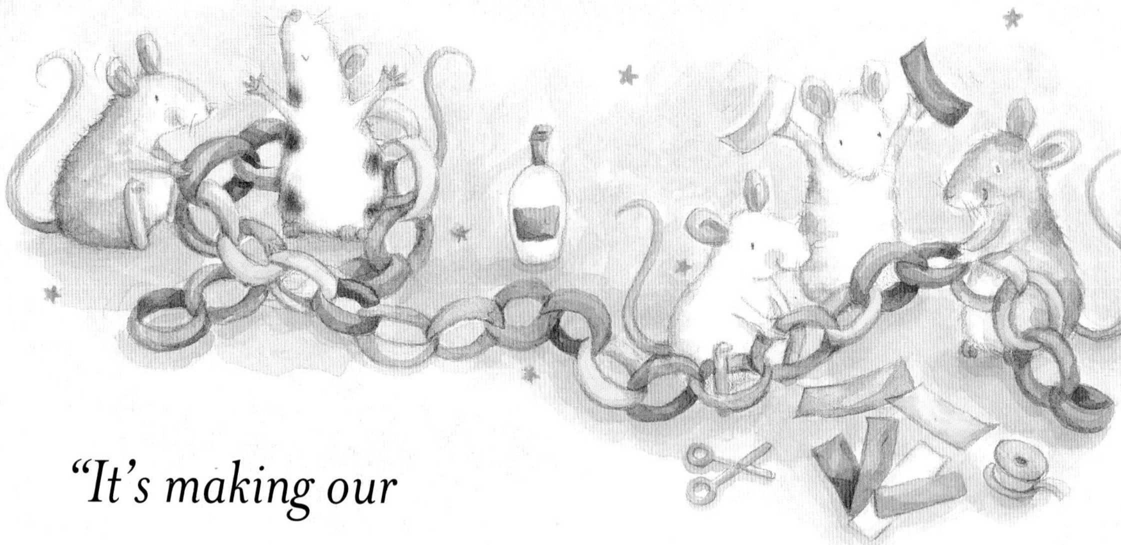

"It's making our
own decorations,
From ribbon and paper and glue.
The magic's in sparkles and glitter,
And colorful
paper chains, too!"

"It's hanging the tree lights," says Daddy,
"That twinkle and glow through the night.
It's pinning the star on top of the tree—
The magic of Christmas shines bright."

"At last, it is Christmas!" smiles Mommy.
"We're together, in one happy house!
Sharing and feasting and opening gifts—
The magic is love, Little Mouse!"

Our long, happy day is now over;
The silvery moon starts to rise.
"Have you had fun?"
Mommy asks Little Mouse.
"It was magical!"
Little Mouse cries.

Mommy Mouse smiles
as she hugs him,
"The magic's in all that we do!
With loved ones and friends,
all together we share
A magic that lasts the
year through!"